# Comfort

Imagine a place where you feel comfort – a place that makes you feel safe and happy.

Peaceful Panda Says:
"Lay with me in my mountain home in China.
Everything is fine at this moment.
I feel comfort sitting here."

I couldn't help staring at the pretty black and white bear cub. She was so unique and beautiful! She seemed to smile as she spoke again...

"Do you know that pandas are the national treasure of China? We are one of the most rare and loved animals in the world. We are unique in the way we look – we always have black and white color, but no two are alike – we all have our own special markings. This is our identity – who we are!" I reached out to touch Ping Ping's fur – it was very thick, soft, and oily! I saw that her fur protected her from the cold weather – it was like wearing a raincoat that makes the rain and snow roll off.

# Pandas and Me

I love to learn by looking at books – books on people, books on special places, and especially books on animals. One day, I picked up the most interesting book and I saw a picture of an incredible black and white bear called a panda. It brought a smile to my face – it was the cutest animal I had ever seen. I wanted to learn more. All day, visions of the panda played in my mind over and over again. At bedtime, when night drifted in, I was still thinking of this mysterious bear.

Suddenly, mist seemed to surround my room as I was swept away to the far off lands of the Chinese mountains. Instead of wallpaper, there were bamboo leaves. Instead of a bunk bed, there was a mossy border. I looked around in amazement at this place before I spotted a large mother panda bear and her cub. The cub saw me and started walking over...

"Hello! My name is Ping Ping," said the little panda cub. I knew that this must be a magical place, because pandas can't talk!

"I live with my mom high up in the mountains of China. It is a misty place filled with clouds, beautiful waterfalls, and tall trees. It's the only place pandas live. We are happy here and feel comfort in our special home."

I saw the misty mountains and tall trees all around. The mist felt cool to the touch and drifted through this special place. In the distance, I could hear a rumbling river. The bamboo trees grew like a green wall all around us. I could understand why they loved this peaceful forest so much.

Ping Ping said, "If you watch my mother, the Peaceful Panda, she will teach you many things, so you can become like us."

# Identity

What makes you special? Think of one thing that you really like about yourself – this is your identity.

Peaceful Panda Says:
"Look at what I can do! I am a precious jewel. There is no one else just like me in the whole world."

Ping Ping turned away for a moment and began to climb to the top of a swaying tree!

I was surprised that she wasn't afraid to climb so high!

She swung from the branches for a moment, squealing with happiness. Then she called down to me...

"When I was very small, I used to watch my mom climb to the top of a very tall tree. This amazed me since she's so big! Panda bears can weigh 300 pounds! She taught me that we can do anything we set our minds to – even climb to the top of the tallest tree."

# Confidence

Think of something that you do very well. It takes great confidence to do this. You are amazing.

Peaceful Panda Says:
"Let's climb to the top of a tree.
I can always do something great.
I am confident that this is true."

I watched as the mother panda bear came over to the tree and Ping Ping came down into her arms. They hugged for a moment and wrestled. When the mother saw that Ping Ping was okay, she walked back to the high grass. Ping Ping spoke again...

"My mom watches out for me very carefully! Panda bears are very good mothers. They are very protective of their babies. When I was born, I was extremely tiny - only about the size of a stick of butter! I was also born with no fur and pink in color – pink as cotton candy! My mother and I stayed in a hollow trunk of a tree.

I will stay with my mother until I am two years old!"

# Giving

Think of something you take care of? What do you like to give to others? It feels wonderful to share our love and time.

Peaceful Panda Says:
"Look at all the ways that I give my love.
I have so many gifts to share with the world."

I felt some icy wind blow and saw snow coming down from the mountaintop. It was starting to get very cold here. Ping Ping sat down on the cold ground – she didn't seem to mind the cold weather at all. Her mother was behind her, chewing on the bamboo leaves.

"I'm learning how to look for our favorite food – bamboo! It's the main food we eat in the wild. We eat for 14 hours a day! We love eating bamboo together and when we are through, we rest under a tree. We are so happy and grateful just sitting under our tree together."

Ping Ping looked at me and said, "It's getting harder for us to find our favorite food here. We may have to leave our home and travel far to find some more."

I wondered if there was any way that I could help?

# Gratitude

Think of all the gifts in your life - all the things you love. You are grateful for everything that you have.

Peaceful Panda Says:
"Let's look for my favorite food – bamboo.
Bring gratitude into your heart.
I am happy with everything I have right now.
I have everything that I need."

I looked off into the horizon and saw that the trees of the forest were very thin. I heard noises and realized that humans were nearby! Far off, there was the sound of a tree being cut down. The animal book had said that the only place pandas lived in the entire world was right here in this part of China. What would happen if the forests were all cut down! Ping Ping saw the sad look on my face and spoke softly…

"Sadly, pandas are disappearing from the world. There are less than 1600 of us left in the forest – this means we are endangered - not many of us left. Our home is getting smaller and if nothing is done to stop this, we will be gone like a dream. My mom says that it is her dream that we will survive with the help of caring humans. There are places right now in China called Panda Reserves where they take care of pandas."

# Dreams

What are your dreams for the future? What do you want to do when you get older?

Peaceful Panda Says:
"When I sleep, I dream of a happy future for all panda bears.
Keep your dreams close to your heart.
You can make them all come true."

I was still thinking of the shrinking forest when suddenly, Ping Ping leaped onto her mother's back and began to playfully roll around! Her mother joined in - stretching, bending, reaching, and twisting all around. I couldn't believe how such a big animal could bend, stretch, and reach so far. The bears were very flexible! They seemed so happy and were having so much fun! Ping Ping got up giggling before she spoke again...

"Panda bears always move around and stay flexible. This keeps us healthy and happy! We love to spend time every day doing flips and somersaults. We are very playful animals. We workout every day! Come join us!"

# Flexibility

Can you stretch like the pandas? It's important to do your Panda Poses every day to stay healthy in your mind and body.

Peaceful Panda Says:
"I love to stretch and move.
I will practice my Panda Poses every day,
so that I will be flexible, strong and peaceful."

I watched as Ping Ping went to a quiet place under a tree all by herself – plopping down on the ground. She sat for the longest time, just looking around with a little smile on her face. After quite awhile, I wondered how Ping Ping could sit there for so long? As if she knew what I was thinking, she spoke...

"Do you know what my name, Ping Ping means? It means Peace. My mom said she named me this because pandas are very peaceful animals. She said we have a very important job to do – teaching people how to be peaceful. We can sit for long periods of time and just be happy. Pandas love just sitting all by themselves. They like being alone. It's easy to do – you don't have to feel bored, sad or nervous. You must have peace in your own heart before you can make a difference in the world."

# Peace

Imagine you're floating on a cloud. You pass by so many beautiful things and you feel at peace.

Peaceful Panda Says:
"I love to sit in the peace pose.
You can have peace in your heart at any time –
just slow down, close your eyes and breathe slowly."

Ping Ping asked me to follow her up the hill to a spot looking down on the valley below. As we sat together, Ping Ping moved her head and listened to all the sounds of the bamboo forest. I also listened, hearing the wind blow, the leaves sway, the birds chirp...

"It's very important to listen. We must learn to hear what our thoughts are telling us and what our world is telling us. If we stop listening, we can get in all kinds of trouble! My mom says that when I have to make a decision, I need to stop, listen and take time to hear what my heart is telling me. I love sitting in the middle of the forest and hearing all the sounds."

# Listening

Imagine you're in the middle of the forest. Take time to stop and listen.

Peaceful Panda Says:
"I love to take time to stop and listen.
Let's find ways to listen better –
by slowing down and listening to all the sounds.
You will learn so much."

I stood looking at Ping Ping and her mother and noticed something amazing – their hearts were shining red and they had huge, colorful wings! I asked why they looked like this and Ping Ping replied that they had earned these strong hearts and powerful wings by being courageous.

"You can make your heart shine and earn your wings by being courageous too. You have seen our world and how special it is! You know it's worth saving. Our only hope lies in people like you! It takes great courage to make a difference in the world. You can help teach people about us. If you want to be a Peaceful Panda Protector, then you can take this pledge."

**The Peaceful Panda Protector Pledge –**

I promise to:

1. See the importance of all endangered animals – like panda bears in the world.
2. Share my knowledge of pandas with people around me.
3. Keep peace in my heart and share it with the world.
4. Find ways to take action and help save the pandas!

# Courage

Think of a time when you were very brave. It takes great courage to do important things and make a difference in the world.

Peaceful Panda Says:
"Stand with me as I make my way through the forest.
I will have to find great courage to make my way.
You can bring courage in your heart by saying
"I am courageous and strong – I can do anything!"

A shining red heart and great wings spread out behind me, as the forest disappeared into the mists below. A new Peaceful Panda Protector was born!

I woke up and jumped out of bed. The mountains and bamboo trees were gone. The roaring river was gone. Now all that was here were the walls of my bedroom, my bunk bed, and my old desk...

I knew that there was still time, and that the great bamboo forests didn't have to disappear like a dream. Not as long as there were people who still cared and would defend the National Treasure of China...the peaceful panda!

As I got up, I heard a quiet voice saying, "Thank you for helping us, and don't forget to spread peace around the world. Your friend, Ping Ping."

**Here's how you can help become a Peaceful Panda Protector and earn your wings:**

- Tell your family, friends and classmates about panda bears and what you've learned.
- Go to Pandas International (www.pandasinternational.org) to learn ways that you can help the pandas. You can adopt a panda or donate money for milk and bamboo.
- Have peace in your heart every day.
- Do your Panda Poses every day.

Once you have acted as a Panda Defender, you can get your wings! Just mail $4.99 for your special Panda Patch to:

**Panda and Kids**
5748 Remington Drive
Winston-Salem, NC 27104

# Peaceful Panda Mobile

1. Photocopy this on thick paper.
   (or on regular paper. Then glue it on cardboard)
2. Color the parts on the copy.
2. Cut the parts out along outlines.
3. Glue, tape or string them together.
4. Tie a string at top of head.
5. Hang it over your favorite place.